T0354654

HER CROWNING FRENZY

A Collection of Poetic Stories

Robin Chappell

authorHOUSE®

AuthorHouse™
1663 Liberty Drive
Bloomington, IN 47403
www.authorhouse.com
Phone: 1 (800) 839-8640

Published by AuthorHouse 04/13/2018

ISBN: 978-1-5462-3774-7 (sc)
ISBN: 978-1-5462-3773-0 (hc)
ISBN: 978-1-5462-3832-4 (e)

Library of Congress Control Number: 2018904644

Print information available on the last page.

Dedication

I would like to dedicate this book to my little piece of sunshine, my daughter, Harmony Grace. You are a BEAUTIFUL God given blessing and Mommy loves you VERY much. You will forever be the driving force behind everything that I even think of doing in my life! No matter what, I will ALWAYS be there for you. I also dedicate this to my loving family. This is for my wonderful mother and father, Susan and Robert. I would also like to thank my best friend and little brother "Bobbie". Without you, I would not have even half of the love, support, and strength that I do today. This is also dedicated to those who helped contribute to my poetry by being my muse. Whether you loved me, used me up, or broke my heart...I most certainly THANK YOU!

The V. Elements

I. Love

"The Troubled Angel"

Beyond the fluffy white clouds in the sky
Past the silver linings and all of the bright lights
Just beyond the twinkling stars of the night
A beautiful little angel sat stuck in her deep thoughts about life
She huffed and she fumed about why she had to go
Down into some unknown place, residing
with souls she did not know
God took notice of her obvious stress and worry
"Aren't you supposed to be gone? You know you really must hurry."
She sighed at His words in pure sadness.
She was so hurt and distraught
Feeling like all of this was madness. She was more afraid than not
"I don't think I want to go. I would rather stay
with you. Even all of my friends are here.
What on Earth is there for me to do?"
She knew that she should not ask questions
But she just couldn't help herself. Why did it have to be *her*?
Why couldn't he send *anyone* else?
God already knew her heart. He could hear
all of the thoughts in her head
He did not blame her or judge her for her fears
He sat her down to have an important talk with her instead
Before he could even begin she crossed her arms and she frowned
"Have you seen the way that she acts? She
doesn't even want me around!

She seems self-centered and reckless. Nothing is ever planned out
She looks to be having enough fun on her
own. There is no need for me
So I should stay right here with you. I am
not the answer that she seeks!"
She looked back at God and was hopeful for concurrence
But instead he took her tiny hand and gave her His solid reassurance
"That is exactly the reason why I am sending you.
Some people need a little help growing up
She doesn't realize her potential and all of the things she could do
Without you her life could become more corrupt
You are the cure for her selfish heart. I know
you won't fail. You are my best!
My little angel with the happiest spirit. More
effective than all of the rest."
She contemplated his motivational words.
Smiling she finally rose and prepared
She needed those words for her doubts and her fears
She heard it gets really crazy down there!
So the little angel packed all of her positivity and love
Along with her happiness and infectious grin
She knew this mission would really be tough
But she could always use a good challenge
She stood at edge of the heavens and handed over her wings
She now was fully prepared to go.
Taking one last look at her heavenly home and the angels that sing
God said "I promise you will be surrounded
by *my* people full of love!"
He planted goodbye kisses upon her face
I will *always* be here guiding you from above
Your mother will give you the beautiful name of Harmony Grace!"

"A Man's World"

"This is a man's world. This is a man's world.
But it would be nothing, NOTHING…
Without a woman or a girl."-James Brown
The darkness and the shadows quickly made their
way around the well-built world of Adamic
There was a gentle breeze in the air as we continued to build
I wiped droplets of sweat from my brow, preparing
to head home after a usual day's work
The siren sounded, dismissing all the men
from their duties and their posts
The usual conversations rang out in the air. Nothing
but endless bragging and boasts of strength
I walked alone. The crowds never really seemed to
welcome me and I was just fine with that
I grabbed my things as my dirty boots pushed away a stray cat
Every day was the same. I prided myself on my work
Stronger than many of the men who only competed
with their egos and completing their mission
I did everything better but I still felt like every
night there was just something missing
My bed welcomed me with open arms and
comfort as I sank into the mattress
I struggled to sleep as my thoughts raced around
and tried to prepare for the next day

As soon as my eyes nearly shut into a deep sleep
against my pillow I became startled
There was a sudden noise and footsteps outside of my window
I silently rose and figured it might be another
drunken night for my best friend Drew
Needing a place to crash again because he could never
find his way to his own home on weekends
That was typical, but this was not a typical feeling that I owned
I cautiously walked to the window and looked
around the depths of my large back yard
In the corner, I spotted a figure looking as if it struggled to walk
I was not yet prepared for the next part
I spotted long flowing hair, wider hips, and
perfect legs wobbling like a newborn deer
I gawked in confusion and in awe as it
began to make its' way more near
The closer it got to the window, the deeper my breathing became
Not only was I confused on what it was, but
I could not even give it a name
I eyed a vision with soft eyes, pouty lips, and voluptuous thighs
Appearing frightened with nothing but a short silk dress and bare feet
Hair cascaded all around its face as soft panicked eyes focused on me
I quickly moved from my window with thoughts filling my head
What is this creature that stumbled upon me? Where was it from?
Why did it have me feeling funny and my heart beating like a drum?
A tiny knock was heard against my window
as I snapped out of my thoughts
I slowly moved back towards it trying to fight
my curiosity, but it won undoubtedly
I peeped out of the window once again and met its gaze
It's as if we automatically connected our minds in an unexplained way
"I need help." It finally spoke in the softest
tone I had ever heard before
A sound so new and mysterious. I just had to have more
It seemed desperate and lost so I decided to dig a little deeper

4

"W-What are you exactly?" I asked the question I longed to know
The confusion and the fear on her face continued to grow
"What do you mean *what* am I? Where am I?"
"You are in Adamic and I'm guessing you
didn't happen to just stop by.
There live no other creatures here who share
your odd but lovely appearance
So, I am guessing you must come from quite far of a distance."
Before I could say the next words, the swaying
began as the creature grew weaker
Smooth legs buckled underneath and I ran outside for the catch
I never took my eyes away as my breathing
intensified when I laid it across my couch
Bright eyes finally shot open and looked around
now that it found some solid ground
Realizing that everything may not be exactly as it appears
It spoke once again
"Am I crazy? Or is it true that there are only men here?"
I looked as if I saw a ghost and I suddenly wanted us to be more close
"I am from Earth. I need to get back there, this was a mistake."
My ears perked up. I had heard about a planet called Earth long ago
But whether it really exists is something that I did not know
She moved closer towards me and I didn't even flinch
"I am a woman. A woman just trying to
get back to where she belongs."
My mouth nearly dropped at her statement, women
did not exist and were not allowed in Adamic
Never had I laid eyes on one until now
There have been stories about these other creatures
whom we called daughters of Eve
One day, one of them left our king betrayed. He grew
angry and immediately sent them all away
I knew that this was crazy and I could possibly be executed for treason
But now that she was here I didn't want her
to leave for some strange reason

5

"I do not think you should be here daughter of Eve."
"Rona."
"What?"
"My name is Rona."
I let her name ring out in my head. Deciding
on whether she needed to know mine
"Rona...I am Jesseph."
She smiled and it made me smile right back.
But what if there are more of her that landed
here? What if we are under attack?
The king made it seem that these creatures were the worst
That all they do is distract us and want to do nothing
but control us from the day of our birth
That they pretend to love you only to always let you down
So, he exiled them and persecuted them and
no longer wanted them around
Here we stay day by day just working to keep our planet pure
This is my first time meeting one and I cannot
say that she seems like a threat
All I can say is that I am feeling quite strange
and practically short of breath
"May I ask how it is that you got here?" I inquired after a long silence
"I made a machine. I am a scientist that has been studying
other planets and dimensions in the universe.
Earth and its violence are out of control
and happens to be at its worst.
My machine can teleport me to anywhere that I would like to
go. But how I ended up *here* is something that I do not know."
I listened intently and became even more amazed as
I stared at her small hands and met her gaze
A woman scientist who also builds machines?
I was beginning to think that these creatures are
not as bad as the king makes them seem.
"Where is this machine now? What does it need for you to get back?
There is no rush, but if the king finds you it can get really bad."

She rose to her feet quickly only to sit right back down
"I first need water, food, and nourishment
before I can even walk around."
Before I knew it, I was on my feet.
Going through my refrigerator and looking through different meats
I whipped up an entire meal for her, amused
and eyeing her every chew
Her energy slowly began to increase as she
gave me unending stares of gratitude
"Now I can lead you to my machine so that I can be on my way."
"Well it's supposed to be bad weather soon, you
probably shouldn't try and go today."
The words left my mouth before I knew it and
she eyed me with a humorous smirk
She sank back down into my couch and in less
than five minutes her lights were out
I watched her as she lightly snored. A
slumbered vision of beauty and peace
Thoughts of violence and death raced through
my head if anyone happened to see
I went to another couch beside her and
before I knew it I also went under
A few hours later there were knocks at my
door, startling me out of my slumber
I cautiously looked out to see who it was and let
out a breath when I saw it wasn't the feds
Drew stood with a look of worry on his face, but I
moved her to my bedroom at the quickest pace
I opened the door as he stood there grinning
like he already knew the secret I had
"Whatever the hell is up with you must be
pretty bad. You never miss work.
I thought you might be hurt."
He moved past me into my house and went straight for a cold beer.
"So, who else has been here?"

He knew me well and was grilling me trying to find out the truth.
We had never kept secrets from each other and
had been close since we were youths
"Why do you ask that?" I moved around as if I were busy cleaning
"Well I know that you're the only one who lives here,
but I see it looks as if *two* have been eating."
I scolded myself for my carelessness and
decided on whether to tell him or not
He already knew that something was up and
I knew he wasn't going to stop
"Look man, you have to keep a secret for me.
This is one that can get me killed."
His eyes widened and I had his full attention
"You know when you talk to me you can always speak what's real."
I slowly walked towards the back and signaled for him to follow me
He placed his beer on my kitchen counter and
walked towards me as I began to lead
She still was in my room and snuggled into my
mattress, snoring lightly and breathing slow
As soon as Drew saw her he looked at me with fear
"Hey man, I have to go."
He slowly moved back towards my front door, shaking
his head and looking down at the floor.
"Drew, it's not what you think, she landed here by accident.
As soon as she's stronger she'll go back to Earth. For now, she's
resting and came to me because she needed nourishment first."
A look of anger and fear decorated his face.
"Do you know what can happen to you as long as she's in this place?"
"Yes! I know the consequences very well, but she is not a danger
and quite an interesting image. I don't understand why we
should stay away or why we even have those laws in place."
"Because she'll probably just end up betraying you just
as badly as the king was betrayed. The laws are made
for a reason. To protect us and live better days!"

"Well maybe not all of them are the same! We cannot have
laws in place because of the actions of *one* woman!"
I was exasperated and frustrated by this fear that the
others seemed to have for these creatures all because
of the actions of one. It made no sense.
Yet Drew seemed to be on the king's side and
wanted nothing to do with my defense.
"Just get rid of her Jess…you know the fuckin rules." He stated
through gritted teeth before he slammed my door behind him.
I shook my head and let out a long sigh.
"Is everything alright?" Her voice startled me as she
spoke up from the dark shadows of the hallway.
"I'll be going now. I never wanted to make any trouble for anyone.
I just landed in the wrong place at the wrong time I guess."
I never turned to face her. "Let's get you
home before I am under arrest."
We slowly walked towards my back door to where
she told me her machine was located.
I looked for more excuses for her to stay, but my
common sense started to become debated
We walked up on a large cobalt gray post
in the wooded area of my yard
It was now covered in leaves and branches
and the sides were a little charred.
I was amazed that what she said was really the truth
and before I knew it the words slipped out
"Please let me go with you."
She turned and faced me. Staring into my eyes as
she let the thoughts run through her mind
"Why on Earth would you want to come to Earth?
It's *beautiful* here and there is no violence, weapons of war, no crime.
Earth is corrupted and will end soon. It's only a matter of time."
I looked down at my feet then at her machine. At this point I really
did not care and felt that I would rather go if she was there.

She read my face and walked closer to me, taking
me into an embrace and kissing me suddenly.
I let out a euphoric breath after she stopped and let me go
I stated the words of my discovery aloud
"*You* are what has been missing."
She smiled and took my hand. And after pushing a
few buttons her beginning became my end.
We bypassed Earth and ended up on a
universe where love was all we need.
Where there was no corruption or any type of rules.
No individuals that were consumed by greed
We lived and loved in happiness, reproducing
with every chance that we would get
I looked at her with admiration saying the same words
at every moment and everything we'd do
"Living in a man's world was once all that I knew,
but I was nothing until I finally met you.

"Wishes"

"I think that it's this way!"
Three women journeyed through the woods by foot
Great explorers and always careful with each new step they took
They knew no limits when it came to possessing great treasure
They would never quit, even if the journey entailed extreme measures
This particular day they sought out the most difficult cave
Deep through forests, over rivers, and vast fields
Past deadly creatures, and barriers of steel
They spotted the cave after ten long days
Although exhausted and sordid from the mission
They celebrated about having their names in
the news and infamous mentions
After diminishing away tough vines and branches
They entered the cave with caution ready
for whatever could attack them
It was dark and it was dank from numerous years of lifelessness
They became apprehensive as they ventured
further and noticed the deadly mess
Skulls and bones ornamented the walls and the ground
Along with large rats making hungry squeaking sounds
They questioned their mission and began
to think it might be time to leave
The fame and treasures they all dreamt of
could soon turn to sorrow and grief
"There is no need to fear, my intention is not to harm you."

They practically jumped out of their shoes,
startled by the hypnotic female voice
"Your journey was treacherous. You all seem famished.
I am sure there is something I can do."
"N-no thanks," stammered one of the women.
"I think we'll just be leaving now."
"But what about your treasures? What about your fame?
I can promise you all of that and more. The
entire world will know your name.
I can grant one wish to each of you and
they will certainly all come true.
Since it is only one I would choose very wisely.
You cannot return here once you do."
The women all looked at each other in thought.
They wondered if this offer was pure
They went off to the side, discussing it amongst
themselves. Feeling skeptical and unsure
Just as they debated back and forth, the figure that
spoke physically appeared before them
Darkly cloaked in a large black hood covering her entire face
Long crooked fingers covered in gloves of black lace
Coldness gripped the cave and the women stood still in horror
It was obvious that she was a witch. Residing in this
cave and granting hungry souls one wish
The most curious one decided to clear her throat,
taking three careful steps forward
"What do we have to do for these wishes?
Everything comes with a price."
The witch cackled a long and eerie laugh. "My
dear, you are wise and you are right.
It all depends on the wish you decide.
What's important to you and what are you willing to sacrifice?"
The women thought for a moment on what exactly they should do
Frozen in terror and wondering if they even
really had a choice or even a next move

"I'm not going to take your lives. Remember it's all about choice
If you wish to decline and leave, there are no hard feelings
I would have no reason to grieve."
The first woman bravely stepped forward
Wringing her hands with her tired eyes lowered
Her one wish was spent on billions of riches,
for she had grown up very poor.
She wanted abundant wealth no limits
With a wave of her hand, the witch granted her wish
Before her eyes lavish diamonds and tons of gold appeared
The witch informed her that when she returned
home there would be much more
She didn't want her to ever think she wasn't being sincere
There would be mansions and fancy cars,
even her name on the Forbes list
The woman rejoiced and gathered her riches in tears and happiness.
Woman number two stepped forward to state her wish
She wished to be drop dead beautiful. She
had never been very attractive in life
Never falling in love or being accepted, she
desperately wished to be a mother and a wife
With another wave of her hand, the witch
quickly granted her wish too
Giving her soft, long and flowing hair and translucent eyes of blue
She now had supple and glowing skin, along
pouty lips the color of a rose
The perfect facial structure along with a perfect nose
Every man would flock to her as if she were magnetic
Every kiss she gave, every word she spoke…men would never forget it
With a whip of her hair and a confident smile
She began to imagine how great her life would be now
So, when the witch coaxed woman number
three to step forward for her wish
She decided not to ask for something selfish
With a sigh of sadness, she finally spoke up

13

"It's my fiancé…it has been pretty tough.
They gave him three months
It seems as if lately nothing has ever been enough
The witch cackled her laugh, "Ah, you want him to live longer?
You'd like me to grant him perfect health so
he'll grow and become stronger."
The third woman smiled meekly looking down at her shoes.
With another wave of her hand, the witch granted her wish too
She told her when she got home he would be at full health
And as if no problems had ever lived there
Doctors would be confused and say his case was miraculously rare
All the women rejoiced from the cave leaving the witch behind
All in agreement that out of every cave in the world
This one was their greatest find
The first woman went home to all her wealth
feeling her life couldn't get any better
She traveled the world, never had to work, and
basked on private islands in sunny weather
She was announced the richest woman in the world
Her wealth even surpassed royalty
But her life became sad and lonelier than the times she was poor
There was not one soul she encountered who showed her pure loyalty
It only took five years for her to succumb to her unhappiness
Knowing the witch's warning, she still ventured back to the cave
Hoping she could ask her to take the wealth back
and she return to her poor old days
Upon entering the cave, the witch was nowhere to be found
In tears, the woman took one last look around
Taking her own life in the cave, she died sad and alone
Adding to the cave's collection of darkness, skulls, and bones
The second woman finally found love. Her
life became unrealistically perfect
Every man told her how beautiful she was, every
man told her that she was worth it
She finally met one in particular who peaked her interest the most

Buying her whatever she wanted, showering her
with love, and traveling coast to coast
She began confiding in him for everything.
She told him about the witch's wishes
Growing interested, he convinced her to lead him to the cave
He had to see if she really meant it
Together they ventured right back to the location
Ignoring the witch's stern words and cautionary limits
The second woman waited outside while he entered the cave alone.
He hoped to make a wish too
The witch appeared vividly before him saying,
"I have been expecting you."
She gave him the instructions that she gave the three women
He stated his wish with pure excitement at the chance he was given
When he walked out, the second woman's
face became pale with dread
In his arms was another equally beautiful woman
He'd wished for his ex-lover to arise from the dead
Not even casting her a second look, they went
back to their lives hand in hand
Leaving her so stricken with sorrow that she could not even stand
She dragged herself back into the witch's cave
Taking one last tearful look around
Taking her own life in the cave, she died sad and alone
Joining her friend amongst the darkness, skulls, and bones
The third woman lovingly laughed with her fiancé,
spending days in one another's arms
Entertaining each other with stories and jokes,
tantalizing each other with charm
They excitedly planned their wedding day
together, picking out colors and themes
She could not be happier and her life seemed like a magical dream
They lived on in love for years and years
With only several bad days and a couple of tears
The witch sat in her cave in annoyed exasperation

15

Wondering why the third woman had not
returned, she demanded an explanation
She usually didn't do this, but she paid the third woman a visit
Her dark figure suddenly cornered her as she
grabbed a snack from her kitchen
The woman didn't seem surprised to see her and
even greeted her with a warm smile
The witch grew even angrier, questioning why she appeared so docile
"It is time for you to sacrifice yourself!
I granted your wish and gave your fiancé perfect health
There is supposed to be an evil ulterior. There
should be some type of dread."
The woman chuckled, sipped her water and slowly shook her head.
"I tell you, evil never prospers or rests.
The day we ventured into your cave your
judgment was not at its' best.
I never stated a wish to you. I made a statement
and you haughtily just finished the rest
My fiancé was never sick, that was something that you just assumed
You have committed so much foul play that
your ego has been consumed.
I never had a wish to make, I am happy with my life as it is.
I was only going to state my fiancé has three
months to come home from the war,
I was *never* going to sell my soul. I have more than I could ask for
You see, when you have love and when you have
God there is no additional problem solver
So, if you would excuse me, I'm casting your
unwelcome evil out of my house
So that I may go back to my peaceful slumber."
The witch screeched out in anger and faded back to her cave
Her figure stiffened into eternal stone where she would remain forever
Eternally trapped and enraged

The third woman slid back into bed with
her husband as he peacefully slept
She lived the rest of her days until she was old
She would always be the woman whose love and
faith was strong enough to take evil's soul

"Dinah"

The door slowly creaked open as I proceeded toward the back
I scurried behind my escort nervously
A scent of desperation and repellant nearly knocking me off tracks
I crept down the dim and narrow aisle
Slowly passing cages full of solemn and downcast eyes peering out
They stared at me so desperately
As if they shared a secret bet on whom would be chosen
"Take a look around and just let me know
when you find one that you like.
They're all a lousy bunch of fleabags!" A
light chuckle. "I'm just jokin'."
I frowned at his comment and kept moving ahead
Some dogs were standing up wagging their tails happily
Others lazily laid in what I guess you would call a bed
I never had a particular breed that I liked
I never really research that sort of stuff
When my feet halted in front of a beautiful blonde golden retriever
It was love at first sight
Her eyes looked into mine silently begging for a chance
But there was no showy presentation of running in circles
No wagging tail or adorable little dance
It was as if she let me know that what I see is it
There was no faking who she was
Like mine, her personality and actions were effortlessly legit
"What about this one?" I inquired curiously

He turned around and slowly looked down
He frowned and shook his head furiously
"That one's got a real attitude problem!" He spat.
To me it seemed like it was all on him certainly
being in the wrong profession
He smelled so loudly of weed he probably thought they were cats!
"Well I'll take her!" I made my decision as a satisfied smile set in
He shook his head and opened the cage but she didn't even sprint out
She delicately crept in my direction with caution
But when she reached me she stared at me as if grateful and proud
"I'll go get all the paperwork." The asshole
finally retreated to the front
When everything was finalized she trotted out beside me
She delicately leapt right into my front seat with a grunt
Dinah was the name I decided to give her. It fit her perfectly
There were no issues with her getting comfortable
She explored my home with curiosity
Never coming off as vulnerable
She had an old soul and only laid around in silence
Following me closely around the house
Learning every room and inch down to a science
She had a courtside view of my dating life too
So, for good reason she really hated Bryan
Every single time that he stepped foot in the house
Dinah could no longer be quiet
That was the most that I ever heard her bark
Bryan certainly did not seem to like it
"Here goes your loud retarded ass dog. Just go and put it away!"
I stepped to her defense every time he grew pissed
"She only does it when you come in, she's my
dog, and you don't have to stay!"
He scoffed at my words and turned to leave
I closed the door right behind him
Dinah let out a low growl as she watched him from the window
I patted her head with a sly grin

So, when Chase came around, Dinah stood her same ground
This time it seemed to be a little worse
When he would visit, she never pissed him off
He never seemed to yell about her barking
Never letting out any scotts
I still quickly realized that he just was not my type
Unmercifully clingy, I grew tired very quick
When I broke things off with him four weeks later
In his head, my words would never stick
He came back around time after time
Candy, flowers, and begging every night
"Please just take me back, I swear that I'll do better!"
I grew exasperated and annoyed beyond my limit
Ignored every call and tore up every letter
When he showed up at my job I knew he needed to be admitted
A restraining order didn't seem to do much
Paranoia set in and I constantly looked over my shoulder
I no longer knew who to trust
One day it stopped like he finally received the hint
Weeks went by and I heard not one word from him
I could barely contain my excitement
I finally went about my life the same as it had been
I could go to my regular places and visit my old friends
Dinah and I had not been out together in a while
We had been out of sight for quite a long time
That certainly was not our style
It was a beautiful and lovely day in the fall
I knew a long walk would make her do more than smile
I grabbed her leash and we headed to our trails
Deep in the forest where Dinah could explore
She immediately recognized her familiar smells
There was a calmness over the earth but Dinah felt more
We eventually left the forest and decided
that we had enough for the day
Riding to the grocery store with Dinah's head out of the window

Just for her, I took the longer way
I left her in the car with the windows down as
I went in and grabbed a few things
Greeting everyone with a smile
When I came to my car, she slept peacefully as if exhausted
I slung my bags in the trunk and dropped my cell phone
I strained and grunted to lean in and get it
In one sudden moment I heard a scream and Dinah growling in anger
I was startled and I looked back in shock
I never would have known I was in danger
Chase followed me and crept up behind me with a knife
With every intention to end my days
Dinah jumped out of the window and
pounced, attacking him in an instant
Ultimately saving my life
I quickly grabbed my cell phone and called the police
Chase groaned loudly and rolled around,
grabbing his chewed-up hand
But I instantly noticed Dinah growing weak
She looked as if she could barely even stand
As I walked to her side a look of horror filled my face
Chase's knife had entered her side twice
I wailed as she slowly dropped to the ground
and her eyes drifted off into space
"You're going to be fine Dinah, the cops are on their way!
Please hold on just a while longer."
The more that I talked the more she grew weak
I cried and silently prayed for her to be stronger
Several bystanders came to examine the commotion
I could barely answer their questions or let out my words
Staying next to Dinah full of disappointment, gratitude, and devotion
She breathed her last breaths right there in that parking lot
Right around the time the police showed
When they cuffed Chase and asked him
questions he acted as if he forgot

He wailed in pain loudly like he was the one dying
At this point I really wished it were true
He was escorted to the patrol car delusional and lying
While I still clung to Dinah uncontrollably crying
I never adopted another dog and decided another one just wouldn't do
She has a nice place in the yard next to my white roses
Still watching over me as I find someone new
They say that dogs are a man's best friend
but Dinah was so much more
She would forever be my best friend that saved my life
And my life was what she died for

"The Flower"

Before I became a man…I was a child
Neck deep in irreparable arrogance
Lashing out in anger and lacking in compassion and sense
Immaturity consumed me and a bottomless future doomed me
I walked the Earth as if I owned it
Women were always there at my beck and call
But for their unconditional love I could never fall
It was despised
No matter how many times I heard their same desperate cries
Love did not exist to me any more than a blind person could see
Nobody had the power to move me
My heart had grown harder than concrete
I quickly dipped into The Three Legged Monkey
A local bar that I seemed to like
After ordering a double whisky I was surprised and amused
The bouncer controlled what was only the third fight for the night
I turned my gaze to a woman standing not too far
A vision in blue was posted only a mere ten feet down the bar
Her sexy stare met mine, which was perfectly fine
I grabbed my drink and headed over to finally speak
Before one word slipped out, she lifted her hand to me
"I am not the answer that you seek."
Inquisitive and rejected
My face twisted and I eyed her slowly and vertically
Language escaped not suitable for a lady

Not suitable for anyone
But how could you blame me?
Who was she to not grant me a chance?
I needed my ego to win
As I went in on her she never seemed to break her stance
Her face held an expression of boredom
As if my reaction was predictable
She had a few moments to spare but I couldn't afford them
She coolly walked away as if I were air
Leaving me puffed up like a rooster
Just leaving me standing there
I finished my shots and left ahead of my desired time
None of the little fishes were biting
The luck of the night wasn't mine
I stepped out of the door irritably
Surprised and amused when "cool woman" walked back up to me
Without another word she handed me a small box that held weight
Then she vanished just as quickly as she came
Ignoring my loud requests of "WAIT!"
Skeptical and nervous I turned the wrapped box in my hand
Not patient enough to play guessing games
Not patient enough to understand
Skeptical and nervous were also the words
What if it was a bomb or some poison?
Something I felt like didn't deserve
Still a small voice told me to humor myself
Deciding I would take it home
I sat it on the top of my shelf
Walking past it pretty cautiously
I decided not to share this news with anyone else
This is pretty dumb
But my feelings were numb
I decided that I would just chance it
I snatched the box back out of its place
As I held it I still began to pace

I slowly unwrapped the paper
Which held a small note
Possible instructions that I am guessing she wrote
"Place me in your world's darkest place
Take care of me and keep me safe."
I scoffed at the vague instructions I read
Tossing the note to the side and sitting on my bed
The box had another smaller box contained
The scariest part that on top was my full name
I breathed slowly and removed the box
Expecting more little secrets and tricks
Like a puzzle or a faulty lock
Instead, inside there was the saddest looking seedling
I'm guessing it was the seed of a flower
But abundant attention is what it was needing
The seed was a vibrant purple and green
Smaller than a quarter and no larger than a bean
The sprout was wilted and leaning to the side
And my curiosity I could not hide
I was not a damn gardener
What did I look like trying to nurse a flower?
A sad ass flower a crazy woman gave me
I stuffed the box in my underwear drawer
and poured a glass of brandy
My phone awakened my tired body at 7 a.m.
My morning wood greeting me aggressively once again
When I opened my drawers to dress my body down
I tried to jerk it open with an annoyed frown
Something had it stuck
And I'm thinking...*what the fuck?*
But my surprised eyes soon realized exactly what it was
The tiny seedling was now larger and stronger
Filling my entire drawer
It now had limbs
Along with promising bulbs on the ends

I cannot lie, I was amazed
Whatever magic this was had my mind dazed
I slowly reached down to find another small slip of paper
Contained in one of the bulbs as if it grew there
I looked around my house nervously
Feeling like someone came right in and placed it purposely
Did this chick know where I lived?
I sure as hell didn't tell her
Maybe she was smart enough to break in
But even I knew better
I slowly grabbed the newly written note
Reading the words that were another simple quote
"Place me in a pot and then in a dark room
Water me a lot but do not water me too soon"
I shook my head in amazement
It was something strange and something different
I have no idea why it was something I chose to entertain
Maybe it would turn into money or even a great weed strain
I had no flower pot just lying around
But a medium sized cup is what I found
I found loose soil and housed it inside
I placed it in the corner of my dark guest bedroom for the night
After that night I honestly forgot about it for a while
I worked, I partied, and frequented bars for two days
Sporting a million-dollar smile
Three days later I walked in to clean up
It was wilted once again looking neglected and extra rough
I remembered what the note said, grabbing several cups of water quick
Even after only a mere five minutes it no longer looked as sick
I continued to pour water until I saw that it perked up
Breathing a surprising sigh of relief, I figured that was enough
At that point I realized that I cared
The thought of this rare plant wilting away had me scared
Every night I decided to nurse it more
Checking in on its health and making runs to gardening stores

It began to bloom so vibrantly
I could have sworn that I could see it breathe
Intricate petals of purple and blue
Brought forth more blossoms full of brighter hues
I could not describe its smell
But it was hypnotic and loud as hell
Every chance that was granted to me
I breathed in its scent and it lifted me
But no matter how beautiful and no matter how bright
I never removed it from its place or brought it into the light
There were days that it seemed stubborn and fought against me
Its limbs brushing against me irritably
Then there were moments I practically felt embraced
Realizing I hadn't even gone out for days or visited my favorite place
Weeks later a new note unfolded from the leaves
I wasn't even surprised anymore and smiled as I prepared to read
"You have brought me light even in the dark
Watered me, nursed me, molded me into art
You thought as a child and your future was bleak
I can finally say I am the answer that you seek
Take me into the light and put me under the sun
One is all you need and I am the one"
I wasn't sure what this message meant but followed its directions
Picking up the large flower I had nursed into perfection
Delicately I took it with me outside into the sunlight
This time it didn't struggle or try to put up a fight
I began to walk away and leave it there but
a voice soon called my name
I thought I was imagining things or that my mind was playing a game
But then I heard a repeat
I finally turned around for the source I seek
I set my eyes on the most beautiful woman I had ever seen
With a face of gratitude and bright eyes so serene
I slowly moved toward her shocked and confused
She softly touched my face

27

"I have been waiting for you"
I could not even speak and just stared at her in awe
What was the woman's name? Where did she come from?
She took my hand and for once I never let go
I cared for her and now she cared for my heart
Teaching me things about love
Things that I once did not know
They say flowers never bloom in dark rooms
But I would beg to differ with a smile
Before I became a man, I was a child

II. Heartache

"Saboteur"

He said, "What the hell are you talking about?"
Exasperation flowing from his mouth
She sat in the corner like a flower in the dark
Feeling imperfect and hopeless, yet all he saw was art
Without another word she rose and left without goodbye
For the hundredth time she declined his
love. He would never know why
Like a wild unbridled horse, taming her would never occur
But when it came to whom he wanted, he always seemed so sure
One week it would be that she was afraid,
the next she would be like a mirage
At any sign of true love and happiness, she was an expert at sabotage
Like a never-ending race, he met her back at the beginning every time
When the guns shot off, he would pace himself.
Determined, he would slowly incline
Letting her know in every way that what he felt was more than real
Like a thief in the night dressed in all black,
it was her heart he just had to steal
"Stay with me and please don't leave. Girl you know I got you."
She heard that line so many times, her belief was beyond destitute
And just like the many times before she
found reason to leave him behind
No matter how many times she would return
or how much he was on her mind

This week it's that she just isn't ready, next
week she would say he's the cause
At any sign of true love and happiness, she was an expert at sabotage
Like the worst Monday at the start of the
week, he went right back to her again
Pure confidence in his execution, he just
knew that one day he would win
"I obtained the moon for you and will get whatever else that you
need. All I ask is for this one chance and that you just stay with me."
She scoffed at his efforts and left once again.
Nothing he did would matter.
This time she claimed that he went too far. How
did even get the moon without a ladder?
So he sighed and went away to return with the sun
But the gift of the sun was still not the correct one
He thought it would brighten her days and make her see the light
Just like every other day, she put up another fight
Like the heartless would say, love never paid her debts
Love only caused more issues just like all of the rest
They always seemed different and true every time
Only to disappoint her with endless and creative lies
"I'm not everybody." He often said.
Hammering his statements in her heart and her head
But every time, she collapsed as if it were
an atomic bomb that he lodged
At any sign of true love and happiness, she was an expert at sabotage
One day she stepped out of the darkness to seek his presence
The same presence she avoided as if he were her peasant
She looked left and right, she searched up and down
But when she searched every corner, he was nowhere to be found
Clueless and lost, she found herself really grieving
"It seems that everybody always ends up leaving."
Days passed by and she still saw no signs. She saw no traces
It seemed he finally left her life
She sent him letters and she sent him presents

Some of the finest gold and even stars from the heavens
There was no response. Not even one thank you
Not even any closure or gestures of gratitude
Feeling frustrated and lonely, she knew of
nothing more that she could do
There was nothing more that she could say
She could not deny the truth
She sent him one last gesture of a beautiful flower she grew
From the darkness and beyond the cracks of the earth
It was very unique with immaculate beauty and worth
Wrapping it up in hand sewn ribbons of silk
She knew if this didn't do it, then nothing else will
Days went by and her ego got no massage
At any signs of true love and happiness she was an expert at sabotage
In her corner of darkness, she sat for days
and cried tears that created a river
As time went by, day by day, it only grew stronger and deeper
One day she looked up and saw his ship float
right to the corner where she sat
Breathing sighs of relief, she finally realized his love had true impact
He walked up and took her hand where she stood
He kissed her with more passion than anyone ever could
She stepped forward to join him but he abruptly blocked her way
He said, "I did not come to stay and I know how you like your space."
She pleaded and she begged with him to give her one more chance
But he turned away her efforts and shot down her advance
For all he knew, everything she would do could all be just a facade
So he sailed away into his own space as she
drowned in the tears of her sabotage

"Sideways"

Twilight commences as we relieve our senses
Reflecting on days unappreciated
Full of complaints and feeling irate
The calm of the storm brings the smell of rain
We stare at each other but it's just not the same
As we touch and hug each other, the feeling is very faint
I grow tired of rants. I grow tired of pain
Nights are full of headaches
Aleve barely able to relieve
There are suspicious conversations you try turning into make believe
Cautious with your words while bearing eyes that could cut steel
I wrestle with the crazy thoughts of exactly what I could feel
What could you know? You made us this way
How could you fix it? What would you say?
"All I want to do is grow with you." I mutter
"What did you say?" You ask
"I don't think that I stuttered.
These feelings that I have for you are coming to an end.
The motives for your future can no longer blend.
We seem to exhaust each other and I don't think that it's fair.
Your heart just seems to be neither here nor there."
I straighten my posture. I get it together.
I must be cut throat and dry, even in the stormy weather
The thunder rumbles low as you stand there amused
Rain soaks the window panes as I stand there confused

The glare of pale light brightly hits your handsome face
You eye your cell phone nervously and slowly begin to pace
You begin to gather your thoughts. You begin to gather your clothes
My heavy heart begins to race against the
path that I righteously chose
"You know that I have to go." You state defiantly.
Nearly jumping out of your skin, for the fifth time your phone rings.
I lay back in defeat and just stare at the ceiling
"I'm about to get out of here. For us there is no feeling."
Staring down your nose at me as if I am the villain
"She's catching on." You continue. "She knows something is wrong."
I roll my eyes and turn my back. My signals of dismissal
You walk away with no more words to say
Pocketing the condom that you wrapped in tissue
You let yourself out as always. Leaving behind your scent
I know that this will never end as I smile at our time spent
The screen on my phone lights up and I pray that it is you
I roll my eyes and answer without surprise
"Hey girl! How are you?!"
I could practically feel her tears through the phone
As she sobs that she is done and finally leaving you alone
She knows there is another woman and just does not understand
I look around as I calm her down
Knowing I would never stop fucking my best friend's man

"For the Next"

We do whatever we want. Him and I
I listened to the crickets and the wolves howl at night
Much more than the lies and how the other women criticized
They were just mad and jealous of me and my privilege
The lighter color of my skin and the
beautiful clothes he adorned me in
Never having to work hard or bake in the sun
I knew I was the only one with that leverage
My dark browns drowned in his crystal blues
He lay in my room exposed and staring
I wondered why I was the one that he decided to choose
He ran his large hand through my thick sandy brown hair
His fingers traced my light brown skin
Inappropriately spending our time like money
Thick thoughts and sweet nothings whispered slowly like honey
By now, Mistress knew better than anyone else
Every night she slept alone. Quiet and out of sight
She would never dare embarrass herself
But at times she embarrassed *me* out of spite
"Your skin is quite lovely." He broke our drawn-out silence
I smiled and threw my long arm around his neck
Inhaling his scent and basking in one of his many compliments
I snuggled between the soft and crisp white sheets
I did not want to be anywhere else but here
I just knew that he truly cared about me and was being sincere

Early the next day I annoyingly swatted a gnat under the blazing sun
I looked beyond the depths of black slaves and white cotton
As I sat and chatted with whom we all called the eldest one
As soon as she saw me, she eyed me slowly
My mother and father were gone since birth
She was the only one who would thoroughly know me
"I haven't seen you in quite a while."
She hung her clothes and produced a weak smile
I knew that she knew and I didn't even need to explain
She knew everything
I sat in front of her cabin delicately
"Nice new linens." She murmured slowly.
I cleared my throat and made random conversation
"How are your hands?" I finally spoke.
"I does what I can and I manage." She started pacing.
I stared off into the distance with him on my mind
Not noticing her worried and tired face
Taking me into a sudden embrace, I became confused
"There is something important that I really need to show you."
She stated these desperate words before pulling at my arm
Taking me past the creek and dragging her old shoes
It was too hot for all this nonsense but I was curious
Looking back towards the plantation longingly
I knew if he thought I went missing he would be furious
I quickly pulled away from her saying that I needed to go
"It won't take long, you're too far gone. There
is something that you *must* know."
Ignoring her, I quickly darted back toward the big house
Deciding that I would speak with her later
Everything was quiet as a mouse so I crept toward his room
Taking in his scent as I slowly walked in
Through his window I could see the full moon
"Oh, he's not here child." From behind me, Mistress spoke
Voice full of angry disdain, yet she spoke mild and low
I stared at her pale face as she slowly inched closer

She inhaled slowly as she eyed my physique
Taking in the appearance of my skin and hair as if inspecting me
"This will soon be over, you certainly don't have long.
No matter how good and passionate you
are, your bond is not that strong."
"That isn't what he tells me!" I blurted the
words before I could take them back
I stood strong and braced myself for the blow of an expected slap
To my surprise, all she did was chuckle.
"You actually think you're better than the others?
Than me? You're more stupid than I thought!
Why do you think that I turn a blind eye and don't act so distraught?
None of you are *ever* special. Only here just
for a trial. Don't believe me?
See what happens when you end up telling
him that you are with child."
I may have been black, but my face turned pale.
She slowly walked off with a smirk
I shook my head and I fell to my knees
Sobbing in to my new silk skirt
A few hours later he stumbled right in
Smelling loudly of moonshine and a few other sins
As he began to grope my body I already knew what to expect
I just stood there frozen in thought deciding not to say a word yet
The following day led me right back to the eldest
I was curious about what she wanted me to see yesterday
This time I would accept it
"How long have you known?" She asked while taking a drink.
"I wasn't sure, but I figured there was something wrong with me."
I gnawed at my fingernails and began to deeply think
"Well you should be ready now." She rose out of her chair
"Ready for what?" I asked anxiously
"Don't worry. I will take you there."
So back through the woods we tread in silence
This time, I did not pull away

This time, I felt that I needed to know
This time, I needed to feel safe
We came to a small opening in the woods
Where rocks and stones lay quite strategically
As if placed there intentionally
"Where are we?" I asked out loud.
"SSSSHHHH! Girl you better respect the dead."
She finally replied after carefully looking around
"This is the place that I needed to show
you. The most forbidden ground
What you have with Master is dangerous. You're on eggshells everyday
And if you don't get out now, I'll say it loud;
you'll be right where these rocks lay.
This one here tried to run off. She didn't make it very far
She fought hard until he caught her off guard
That's why he has that small facial scar."
"This one here," she pointed to another stone,
"she was caught writing a letter.
Another slave on the plantation loved her better
So now here her rock and her ashes lay
Master found another pretty slave girl the very next day."
My mouth dropped wide open as I stared and I viewed
But I could utter not a word as I let her continue
"This one here was in your situation
Thinking they would be happy together
But when she told him her news there was no elation
She wanted to keep the baby but he wouldn't let her
So, he also got rid of her presence
Brought her right down to this creek
Even as she begged and struggled for her life he just laughed at her
Already had another slave girl by the last breath that she breathed."
The warm tears streamed slowly from my eyes
I listened to the cold acts that he had been doing
I could not accept that I could be next
My name and legacy would be in ruins

39

I slowly backed away in anxiety and fear
Knowing that the worst was drawing more near
"We are nothing to them if we have no benefit.
Merchandise is all we are and he makes sure that he profits."
I stared at her sadly and in angst
Mere thoughts of ways I could escape to live
Yet, unfortunately this story's end is the same
He eventually extracted my existence
I was the only one there was to blame
Poisoning my food was his only difference
Right after mistress spilled the news
Love is incapable of living in their hearts
If you are my replacement and happen to be reading this letter
Just know that you have only a temporary part
He only wanted you because you were next
You were never better
-Sincerely,
Unknown

"Hypothetical"

I am screaming on the inside
Darkness surrounds me and I am still
My heart could freeze an entire lake
Nobody knows that I am completely empty
That there is nothing more I can bear to tolerate
I sit on my bed in deep meditation
Thinking on my life in a constant rotation
Would you save me if you knew?
Maybe I was blind to your point of view
Guess I wasn't what you expected from me
I was not enough for you
I am the disappointment you didn't notice
The overlooked depression that filled the room
As you only sat and pointed
Judging as if you were God
Or as if your dirty spirit was anointed
But I know you
I know just what you are
Now that I am here my feelings don't matter
You willingly reopen every scar
You adorn me with more wounds
And now my heart no longer has room
So the day that you walk that tearfully long aisle
Slowly marching towards a fancy box
Surrounded by flowers stretching a mile

Listening to a preacher speaking a eulogy
That's most likely written for everyone else
Since he knows absolutely nothing about me
As your tears flow in puddles and your head bows in shock
And you swear that you're in a dream
A dream that you constantly wish you could stop
Words that you said run a marathon in your head
What could you have done better?
What are some encouraging words you could have said?
You didn't recognize the signs
You never saw this in my eyes
Why didn't I ever say anything?
Why haven't you even seen me cry?
Yet on my bed, alone at this very moment
I can barely catch my breath
Hyperventilating in rivers of tears searching for an inch
Any brightly small sliver of hope and inspiration
Words to gently change my mind
To steer my promising dedication
Clutching pills created for a more sound sleep
Was my promise to rest peacefully and eternally
To rid myself of a pain so deep
That I have convinced myself the world is better off without me
But everything is just words
Words said with no "hard feelings"
Just as everything can sometimes be hypothetical
Maybe I am only hypothetically speaking
…Maybe

"Dirty Secrets"

Time is stopping
Everything that was said exclusively
Every discreet secret and lie that was told
Finally began to grow old
Practically predictable
They would be subtle at first
Growing into a pink elephant in the room
Dying of unmerciful thirst
You took an inch of my character and my morale every time
I knew it just was not in me
I knew I did not need it in my life
The first time that we did it was a rush
The first time it wasn't like I was forced
You never pushed
I just watched you with intent curiosity
Motivated and intrigued by your unemotional abilities
The first woman never even saw it coming
She looked happy and chatted on her phone distractedly
She was perfection
A target lacking the gift of awareness and observation
So, I did not think when I watched your knife enter her skin
That there was any type of noted acquaintance or relation
I only watched as her face intricately changed
From happiness…to fear…to surprise
Then I finally watched as from her eyes, life drained

Your eyes held no compassion, yet your face showed you were satisfied
My interest could not be restrained
Even when I told the authorities the prepared and scripted lies
You waited for months before the next act
You contemplated on how to attract
Attract the attention of a beautiful charismatic female
As she sat poolside at the hotel where you worked
Relaxing and sipping a cold ginger ale
Her life looked normal and healthily served
As if she owned not one care in the world
I was instantly insecure as I stared dreamily at her pretty naked feet
And as she screamed out like a frightened little girl
"Drag her over there!"
You always ordered me around and I carried out every demand
I figured I wasn't wrong and I never committed the murders
If we were ever caught they would surely understand
Little by little and day by day
Our collection added up in a beautiful way
Collecting gorgeous souls who probably had many goals
I would laugh when you would tell me I was a natural
My adrenaline built on one occasion
A woman that was literally drop dead gorgeous
Blended together with Black, Indian, and Caucasian
She was terrified, and I watched hundreds
of lovely tears flow from her eyes
I tried to wipe them away and convince her that she was safe
She wouldn't let me touch her skin
So lovely and golden, I was desperate to be her friend
When her curses and her foul insults shot me down
My disappointed rejection was blatantly profound
And there he was
He could smell it all over me
The sadness taking over my face
The potential that I would never see
I watched as her bound wrists turned a crimson red

Redder than the blood that seeped from the blow to her head
He slowly strolled up behind me
Sliding the knife right into my left hand
Leaning down towards my ear
He said, "This one's yours." Knowing I'd
follow his indirect command
When she began to scream and called me a bitch several times
It was as if a hidden switch flipped on inside my mind
Bright colors flooded my entire view
The room and its contents became so misconstrued
Before I knew it, my left hand came down
Landing in the middle of her chest as she made sputtering sounds
First there were five, then ten, and then twenty
Enough to her body and enough to her face
Enough to compromise her once flawless beauty
I began to breathe heavily as I fell back
Slinking away from my heinous act
The sound of applause came from behind my back
He rested his hand gently upon my shoulder
I panicked now that I was back in my normal state of mind
I panicked now that I felt sober
The knife fell from my hand and a sob escaped
Yet adrenaline rushed through me at an alarming rate
What have I done?
This is supposed to be *his* idea of fun
He let out a chuckle and lit an L
While billions of thoughts raced in my head
Like what it's like to be damned to an eternal hell
After that day I was never the same
I didn't even want to watch anymore
I cringed with fear and nausea whenever he would call my name
Then the moment came when I had enough
The day he killed three at one time
It was just too much, and it wasn't cool anymore
He grew too aggressive and they were always demeaned

The faces of our victims were adorning television screens
Every time that I saw them I could still hear each of their screams
As if it were their signature
As if it labeled their horrific deaths and lost dreams
I attempted to make a run for it
I darted for the door desperately
It was as if he expected me to break
Grabbing me back predictably
Now my screams were added to his collection
I struggled to break free from his grip
The more I fought the more amused he became
He kissed me with force, but I knew it was the last
He practically bit a hole in my bottom lip
When I broke free once more a sharp pain to
the head crashed me into the door
In dizziness and confusion, I dropped like a bag of rocks
Never knowing the twisted fate that he had in store
When I finally awoke I thought that it was raining quite hard
Or that someone above me was shuffling a brand new deck of cards
My feelings grew more hurt as I realized my doom
Realizing it was the sound of dirt hitting
against my wooden boxed in tomb
It felt like death and darkness staring into my face
It felt dirtier than an abortionist's room
Dirtier than all of the crimes we committed
Dirtier than a New York hobo's linens
Dirtier than the photos in a corrupt politician's phone
And just like the fate of such, I could only lie here all alone
There was no turning back as my world grew pitch black
Right along with our endless lies, he unemotionally buried me alive
The sound of his grunts and heavy breathing
were the final sounds that I heard

I didn't fight, or try to claw my way out,
nor scream in an attempt to deter
My sins consumed me in the way that he groomed me
I breathed my last breaths and whispered my last word
"Father"

III. Passion

"Snaps"

A room full of rhythm and blues
Saturated conversations that hold no volume
Eyelashes that bat and sexy people who scat
Immediately feeling out of place in my solo space
The loneliness of the night carried me to this universe
Filled with funky hairstyles and mellow moves
Everyone around me seems full of promising grooves
I have no cool. No purpose but to listen
A pointless mission still holding wild expectations
As I sit with lack of confidence
Souls around me exposing themselves raw
I am self-conscious on whether I even have on my good bra
I was an alien whose shit just happened to crash land
I take another drink. I pick at absolutely nothing on my hand
Eyes down so low that I almost missed the arrival
The confidence of your walk floating to the stage
I imagine that I am imagining you actually meeting my gaze
Maybe you are looking through me or past me
Or behind me at the beautiful yellow bone
But as our eyes locked again I start to drown
In the depth of light browns undressing me
You got me thinking why? And how?
I fidgeted and squirmed beneath your silent indiscretions
Heavenly thoughts begin to fill my head. Your face is a blessing
The intensity of your gaze is unbearable

I want to run or hide myself but it is impossible
Your broad shoulders are squared beneath beautiful low wavy hair
Plump lips that look sweet finally begin to speak
If my attention were a cup it would certainly overflow
Like a firefly on a summer night, my skin begins to glow
I feel like you know, but my secret it safe with you
Aware of all of the self-control I am certainly about to lose
As passionate words escape your lips I get chills all over
Flushed with the color red down to the bone
Everyone else fades from sight as if we are here alone
Never taking your eyes from me, you recite the sexiest poetry
Licking my brain. Sucking the g-spot of my soul
Stroking my ego. Riding my heart strings extra slow
My breathing is heavy with every small flick of your tongue
The spine of my back is arched, and my full lips are very parched
This moment is sensual art. This night has not been wasted
Under your stare I sit in my chair and I bravely take it
I couldn't even fake it and I'm not even going to try
I sigh. Clenching my legs together extra tight
My palms begin to sweat, and we haven't even met
I breakdown with embarrassment, you read between my lines
As if you have known me for years. As if you are mine
I am not fine. I am confused on this
entrancing game I am about to lose
As you come to your close I am now pulling at my clothes
Feening for more I find the strength to rush to the door
I am clumsily fumbling for my keys. Is there a closer exit?
Is there a faster way to leave?
The drop of cool that I had expired and went bad
All eyes were now on me speaking on the obvious climax I just had
At you I could not look back. I would never even be the same
As my feet quickly shuffled back to my car
I was feeling more than lame
So, imagine my surprise as my confidence got a rise
When I hear you ask, "So tell me, what's your name?"

"The Visit"

I lay still in the heat of the night
Thoughts of him racing through my head
I understood why he had to be away from me
I really wished that he were here instead
Thousands of miles and too many months
My patience was becoming paper thin
I questioned my loyalty and future for us
I was not sure that I could do this again
So as I rolled over to my other side
I gasped in surprise as I faced him
In all of his presence and all of his glory
My broken heart came alive and started racing
I smiled at him. He smiled at me. Never asking any questions
Not really caring how this was possible or if it was pure deception
He finally answered my silent inquiry
"You are only having a dream. I can't stay for
very long. Nothing is as it seems."
Before I could speak he deeply kissed my lips
I melted into him like ice to the heat
Consumed by him as he eased lower and he consumed all of me
Wetness was released but my heart he had achieved
I embraced every moment like death was near
As we floated to the ceiling I still showed no signs of fear
He took my body as his precious possession
I trembled from the glorification of this reception

High from his love and high on my sky lights
He gave it to me like I did something wrong
Every bit of it felt right
He whispered in my ear "Hold on me to me."
I grabbed him and obeyed more than willingly
He rocked my body to a depth so deep
When my moment hit I could not imagine what this could be
I did not know when I would have this moment again
And prayed that it would never ever have to end
But unfortunately it seems that all good things do
I had to let go and could not deny the truth
As he brought me back down and my breathing calmed
He wiped away a tear from my face
He apologized for not staying long
He kissed my lips again so sweet and so light
Within seconds he was gone within the blink of my eyes
So once again I would have wait. My fantasies had no limits
I smiled brightly with the morning sun
As I awoke from his surprise visit

"Expectations"

Always so eager to feel you inside me
To grasp a euphoria only you can provide me
The softness of your lips is more inviting every time
I imagine our pleasure inclining
Inhaling your scent and your presence for days
Inside the wetness of my excitement is where you play
You suck the taste of my skin as I glow from within
I moan out my approval in melodic hymns
You push me to the edge. You let me in your world
I never want to escape and want to be your one and only girl
Your only ultimate drug that you just have to have
So grab a hold of my waist. Make every small moment last
The grandeur of time is that right now we have plenty
Please take your precious time with every orgasm that you give me
I want to repeat your name over and over
again as if you do not know it
Smack redness on my ass like I am a fan of the crimson tide
Pull back my thick hair while the waves of my thickness you ride
To an ecstasy of pure therapy that I never want to hide
Nobody else could ever give me this feeling that I need
Or make me so wet without even touching me physically
Every wish and every dream revolves around only you
Giving me everything that I want
Doing things I never expected you to do

"Melanin and Clover"

Slanted light brown eyes bore a hole into my soul
I watched as she slowly floated toward my atmosphere
Like those tiny specks in the light that catch your eye
Right in the corner and in the middle of a daydream
She was such a vision and cooler than Earth's coldest winter
With a smile warmer than a burning fire's fading embers
I could tell this was the official start
Something new was brewing inside of my world
A world of mundane class schedules
Failure, success, and expectations are full of endless black holes
But she changed all of that in just one moment
With but one way and with but two simple words
"Got smoke?"
I suddenly looked up into the light but deep browns of her eyes
With a concentrated effort to not creepily stare
And to answer with words that would not cause me to choke
"What?" I asked with surprise.
She caught me completely off of my guard
Knocked me off of my feet without even a promise to catch me
Something still wanted me to trust in the hearty laugh she let out
To escape into a world with her
Containing no pointless conversations or overthought doubts
"My uh…acquaintance over there told me you possess the green.
The trees of unadulterated quality and abundant means."
She smirked and eased into a chair across from me

She knew the secret riddle and I looked
over in the direction she pointed
My former roommate smirked at me from five tables down
I already knew her motives
I knew what all of this was about
I lowered my head in silent embarrassment
Yet I was relieved at the same time
I inhaled as her movement slightly lifted her shirt
Swirling her scent into my nostrils which
lifted me and all of my senses
She continued my client riddle so that I knew she was legit
"They may dream of a genie but I dream of Mary
With soft lips of bud so cold and so frosty
So sticky that I cannot move
Possessing waves of euphoria deep enough to swim
Highs full of relaxation and happiness
Lows that all come to dead ends."
I stared into her face
Skimming her naturally kinky and sandy red hair
Blessed with freckles that adorned her
anatomy in more than one place
She spoke of it with her eyes closed
Biting her plump bottom lip like she could just imagine the feeling
Orgasmic feelings that took her to a place I wanted to share with her
My mind was yelling at me right now
Demanding me to say something
Something interesting, or funny, witty and smart
But I am guessing an answer to her question
would be the best way to start
"I have what it is that you seek."
I smiled
Mostly because she practically lit up like every star in the sky
More bounce showed in her demeanor
There was a sexy mischievous look in her eyes
"Meet me at this address at 5 o'clock."

I pressed a slip of paper into her soft and small hand
Grabbing my book I left her standing there
Not another word spoken
As if I didn't care
I sashayed away and had to practically cheer myself on
Knowing I had waited for her to speak just one word to me
I had to coach my mentality not to look back
to see whether she was looking too
As soon as I stepped outside I exhaled deeply
I watched the clouds of my breath hitting the cold air
The hands of every clock grabbed my attention
during the rest of my classes
Her voice played through my mind like a song
I had been waiting to hear that sound for weeks
Never knowing that it would really come true
When 5 o'clock finally hit I made my way through miles
Miles of the lost, the heathens and the smart
As they traveled within their own worlds
I walked into the campus library
Steps and lips more silent than a devoted monk
The sound of my heart sounded like thunder
Then there she was
"I never really come here. I almost couldn't find it."
She giggled sheepishly
As if ashamed that her disinterest in a library was to blame
I slowly brought my index finger to my lip
The universal signal of silence
She obeyed and followed as I brushed past her
I led her to the deeper silence of the study rooms in the back
Their abandonment was obvious
I shut the door delicately as I watched her foot tap
Nerves or excitement?
I finally reached into my bag
A lovely and intricately loud quack
Once our transaction was done I slowly turned to leave

Not another important or meaningful word to speak
"So, what are you about to do?"
Words that stopped me dead in my tracks
Before I knew it, she was journeying with me
Off the campus to my apartment where we could be more free
She made herself comfortable on my couch
As if she had no boundaries and felt right at home
Kicks and giggles filled the room and the entire night
Smoking five L's and feeling more than right
We were finally stoned
And she really was sitting here in my zone
She took another pull then leaned in towards my face
Shooting me with a shotgun of smoke
I shyly let out a laugh and cough
Applauding myself for preventing a choke
This moment deserved something different
Something to remember fondly if it later crashed
I jumped up suddenly and nearly startled her too
"I promise I'll be right back."
Shocked at what I was actually about to do
I darted down the hallway and into my room
Searching through my closet I pulled out a box
One that was hidden deep within the depths of my supply
One that I had not opened and that I was
saving for a moment of perfection
No predictability of rejection
A great friend of mine bestowed this strain upon me
Saying it came from the mountains and soil of a foreign land
In other words, they told me it was great fuckin weed
I decided to roll it up and take this ride
With her I decided it just might be worth it
And even if things don't work out it might be just what I need
So I rolled it up with a smile on my face
Then checked my hair and made sure it wasn't all over the place
I stepped back into the room with the vibe of the Cheshire Cat

Planting myself right back in the spot where I once sat
She looked at me so calm with no signs of irritation or impatience
"You want to come with me?"
I stared into her eyes as if searching for
automatic signs of negativity or doubt
But she didn't question anything
Never asked what the hell I was talking about
"Hell yeah." She responded.
With a smile I lifted the fat blunt that I rolled
Delicately wrapped in a Garcia Vega
I lit it and pulled
Before I knew it we had both completed the entire thing
Practically coughing up our insides
The strain was so good it felt as if it came from another planet
Within moments I felt like I was on one
Her face began to glow like electricity surged through her body
Her hair now resembling a dandelion
I swore I saw her freckles begin to form constellations
So many things going on
So many crazy sensations
"What the hell is this that you gave me?"
Now the questions began
I looked at her with a grin
Our eyes were so low I was surprised we still possessed sight
Next thing I knew we both laid back at the same time
Straight into a poppy field full of vibrant color
The sun was shining across our faces
Melting our realities like butter
Nothing made sense anymore
But then again *everything* made plenty of sense
We already knew where, why, how, and when
Blades of grass blew back and forth in the wind
Swaying as if moved by music
The jazz and blues that we could hear in the clouds
Making deep melodies and playing loud and proud

The air smelled beautiful
The field went on for miles and miles
With only two weeping willow trees in the distance
I never wanted this euphoria to fade
I felt like I could live in the moment for days upon days
Suddenly she turned her head to the side
Staring intensely into my eyes
I stared back and she leaned in
Molding her full lips right into mine
As soon as it happened we lost track of time
From the field there were planets of passion
Galaxies of love and laughter
I embraced it like I embraced her
Saying nothing at all
No words were ever needed
Her body communicated with mine
Speaking in tongues and movement combined
No fears were in existence
Doubts were made unaware
Especially when her clothes were gone
Everything was beautifully bare
In a deep dark room filled with floating fireflies
Her skin glowed
I could no longer hide my pride
I could see everything
Even the essence of her name
Not knowing whether I should call it lucky
Opportunities such as this tend to get ugly
Beauty appeared everywhere
Our thoughts entangled and wondering if we're really here
Things switched to a hire gear
As we floated with the ocean
Matching its' refreshing splendor
Matching its' every motion
The songs we heard were beginning to belong to her

Slow alto notes that touched my soul
Then proceeded to higher sopranos
Rhythm and blues blended with caramel hues
Melanin everywhere
Black lives mattered and we really cared
I could not keep my hands away from her hair
Tugs and pulls
Pulls and tugs
Wrapped around my hand
Treated delicately and rough
This dimension where we stood
Smelled of passion and it was more than good
Now I could do nothing but sing her praises
As we walked quietly through a garden of roses
Snowflakes of powdered sugar all around
Sprinkling the tips of our noses
I watched as she giggled
Her energy never drained
Her intrigue never faded
As she danced around in candy rain
I would forever live this moment in my head
I was certain that it was impossible to fade
Now as I looked around
I finally found the reality of the mess that we made
I had no complaints and welcomed it all
Enjoying the rise if we happened to fall
At that moment I realized her spirit was all I would need
So I made it my intention to keep her around
And to sincerely thank my friend for the weed!

"At-mos-fear"

How on Earth did you find me?
How did I find you?
We were friends
In a world of chaos
Always beaten black and blue
Every time that I saw you chills flooded my anatomy
Dark skin so beautiful and tight like saran wrap
Soft and thick dark lips to match
Eyes sparkled like black diamonds
You were the epitome of a Black man
An adonis
A king in his own right
Full of new ideas and wisdom
Always down for the cause and the fight
We were aware of what was going on with our people
We cried together over their fates
People being gunned down by law enforcement
Lives carelessly thrown away over race
Together we never overcame
Could never look at an iced tea and skittles the same
Fear showered our minds as we walked around
Or when we saw blue blood running through the ground
Attending every protest
Staring at the news in agony
Supporting those who could no longer speak

Your passion made me so excited
Your eyes would make me weak
Buckling my small knees beneath me
Long black dreads cascaded over broad shoulders
A chip rested on them the size of a boulder
Yet you still found the time to shoot me a line
To act as if I never phased you
As you stared at me from the dark corners of your intense eyes
I'm sure it was because at the time I belonged to your friend
What if things would have been different?
I belonged to your partner whose ideas would match yours
Upon our first meeting you also belonged to
a woman who never seemed sure
She never matched your moxie
Could not even match your pride
And when I lay beside the body of mine at night
Your face constantly soaked up my panties and my mind
I would fantasize about your hands
Caressing and touching every inch of my body
Your skin blending in with mine
Stronger and warmer than a homemade hot toddy
Extra whiskey
I imagined you would kiss me
Then tell me we should fight the world together
When I stared into your beautiful face
And my fingers interlocked in your dreads
I felt nothing but safe
Even in the stormiest of weather
I imagined I could be your queen
With our quality and traits blending well together
We would make a perfect match...it seemed
Both of us could be happy and hungry for more
I would always have your back
Looking forward to you walking through the door
My significant other began to notice

Saying that you had eyes for me
I would laugh it off but later I thought
"Is it really me that he sees?"
I grew more interested at the thought
The music that we created together created a stronger bond
Notes filled with quick side glances
Our lyrics oftentimes molding into one
Our situations changed one day when we both became free
The relationships we entertained stopped working out apparently
You finally reached out to me
Not about music, the news, or a favor
Our conversations changed up
We began to put out a different flavor
That's when it all began
The fateful night I finally felt your hands
For two years I had been dreaming
You were the source of my orgasms during masturbation
Now we finally stood alone in a dark room
Staring with very little hesitation
I'm not the girl that does this
The girl that moves from her ex to the friend
The girl that just yells *"good riddens"* to a
life I thought would never end
I still lived in the memories of the past
But shit I wanted you so bad
So I didn't struggle when you pushed me back
And onto your bed I landed
I didn't protest when you slid off my panties
There was no regret or panic
Oh but when your mouth made contact and
you tasted my inner thoughts
When you drank from my flood of excitement
I felt like it started something deeper than I could explain
I felt like it started a riot
Every single touch fulfilled the feelings I had imagined

Every flick of your tongue had me thinking you must know magic
I couldn't make it stop
I couldn't stop coming
And after a while of screaming and writhing I grew tired of running
Embracing the pleasure
A climax that could never be measured
You dove in better than an Olympian
I had no words to shed as I touched your dreads
As I pulled them like the reins on a thoroughbred
Back arching deep as my body still leaked
Then losing my mind when you first entered me
You took my breath and you took my strength
You took away my boundaries and my common sense
In every way imaginable this was the start of an addiction
A drug that would come back to tease me
Every moment that it was mentioned
Weeks could go by and days could go by
Yet we would still find each other and never let this run dry
You practically made me cry
The times I realized you were not ready for me
I understood you weren't the man I imagined you to be
Expectations had to be lowered
Sex was easy but when it came to real time and dates
You would stand me up so carelessly
I knew I deserved better and I knew I deserved more
And I would wait and call and call and wait
While you ignored me and laughed with another date
While you made up excuses you thought would set it straight
I would decline my friend's plans for you
But then would come the day that you still called my phone
And invite me over for our sensual moments alone
I always obliged and I still showed up
I never knew that first moment would lead to a war
Or that one day you would decide it was me you were fighting for
Years later we finally began spend time in public

Enjoying each other's company
It felt like we both loved it
But then one day my mind clicked and it ran around
Making me feel like we were never on solid ground
I needed promises and a bond
I swore you would always just stand me up again
And I would always be left alone
Right after I fell for you to the point of no return
I never wanted to be driven insane
I wanted to protect my heart and my brain
So when I was on the edge I could never jump
I never wanted anyone else so much
But you had already cast the first stone
You never knew that I was made of glass
Every throw broke me down a little more each time
Then came a point where you just satisfied my physical needs
I told myself this was where it stopped
This was all that we would ever be
I used you up
Even during the time you weren't mine
Situationships and relationships got in the
way of what could have been
I asked myself in the darkness when you held me after
Would this turn into five years?
Maybe ten?
Well now it's actually at three
And you sit there and still look at me
Only now the difference is I really don't care what it is that you see
I really don't know what it is that you want
We fuss and we fight
We fight and we argue
About how you can never have your way with me
Words slicing through thick air
You know that I could never fully trust you
So when you tried to show me seriousness

I sabotaged it every time
This time I would stand you up
This time the doubts and the loneliness would not be mine
I would retaliate and show up late
Or never even show up at all
I would say harsh words I never wanted you to hear
I would never even pick up the phone
No matter the actions or the messed up times
All I ever wanted was for you to genuinely be mine
To hold me and say I'm the only one
Not just meet up in fast spurts and have sexual fun
But we lived in those moments
And I felt it all
Especially the days after when I could barely walk
Now the anger and the frustrations that we felt
We took it all out on each other
Only thinking of ourselves
Disappearing and reappearing
Hiding and finding
Kissing and grinding
It all came together and I always had to choose
Always had to contemplate if we walked in each other's shoes
What if we now we're just considered lost fools?
I knew for a fact that *nobody* would ever fuck me like you
Touch me like you
Kiss me like you
Taste the drips of my juices
Help me tear up a room
You possess every ounce of my sexual prowess in your veins
When I masturbate I still find myself calling out your name
Imagining my wetness on your thick lips
Wetness glistening and shining on your thick-
Damn, here it goes again
This has got to be just bullshit
Every time I make the choice to meet you for drinks

I never even deny it
I never even think
When you tell me we can smoke trees together
I float right over to you
No matter the situation
No matter what it could do
I keep letting you back in
How can I explain myself?
Listening to "Ex Factor" by Lauryn Hill
Swooning to "Another Again" by John Legend
You are my kryptonite at night
The towel that I throw in when I've given up the fight
My most satisfying regret
The poison taking over my head and my bed
I get nervous around you now
From fear of doing too much or not enough
Fear of losing you altogether
Fear of just saying FUCK IT
Begging and requesting to keep you around
Now that I am finally found
I think I might even be in some type of love
Or is it obsession?
Is it addiction?
Or could you be my worst DRUG?

IV. Rebellion

"Greenhouse"

I quickly dodged a drone hovering overhead
Sirens whine in the background incessantly
My chest heaves up and down
As I suck in the air polluted by an evil so rare
"I think she ran this way!" A loud voice shouts
I remained still in my space as if it were my shelter
But I knew that I could not stay too long. I knew much better
Easing along the dark wall of the alley
My mission was more than dangerous
It was practically suicide but an adventurous ride
I made my way towards the city gallows
Pulling down my hood over my worried face
I knew in order to make it in time I needed to go a quicker pace
The familiar voice boomed over the city intercom
Chanting my description for the hundredth time
My body was exhausted and peace of mind had never been mine
Down the dirty streets I found my way
Passing children with no homes but engulfed in screen less phones
The year was 2124. The anguish of the world could not be ignored
Living pointlessly each day with the ignorant
I knew I did not belong. I had always felt different
A series of soldier's marching footsteps made me switch direction
With no affection I eased my body past the gallows
Where they hung a young man by his neck
after his last prayer and last swallow

I flinched with anxiety as my cell phone buzzed
I already knew who it would be as I answered on the third ring
"Give it up or your family dies." A rough voice demanded.
My face grew hot at the ultimatum
"Never give it up...no matter what."
I looked into his eyes as he stared into mine
"No matter what they say, no matter what they do.
What I am putting into your hand is bigger than them, me, and you!"
I closed my eyes tightly as I listened to the
words of the man that I loved.
I knew he was right as we lay there that long night
Years ago when he finally trusted me enough to let me know
When he was still around for me to touch, smell, and see
Now because of "them" there is no us.
There is only this secret that he left and me
A secret that he brought back when he returned
From his journey over thousands of seas
I snapped back to reality as the voice spoke again
"I repeat, your family will die in 24 hours
if you do not turn yourself in."
I exhaled as I looked around the forbidden land
Knowing very well that they did not have to say it again
I came upon the only place left in the world that had real green grass
The only place with green trees inside of a greenhouse that still stands
Guards surrounded it like an actual brick wall
I stood tall. I evaluated the situation and contemplated my plan
I looked down lovingly and stare at the small seed in my hand
At that very moment a drone beeped and
began raining bullets towards me
In surprise I ran, which alerted and dispersed the guards
Which were standing not even a distance of five yards
"That's her!" They shout. "Hurry and grab her quick!"
"They'll want her alive much more than
dead, so don't do any crazy shit!"
I spotted a small opening behind the greenhouse

I eased inside quietly and placed my right hand over my mouth
I at least made it to where he told me as I
thought of my treacherous journey
"We know what you have." I remembered their words
My mind went back to the first time that I was captured
I squirmed angrily in the chair under their piercing stares
Never taking away my gaze from the hate in their face
Six of the most powerful beings in the world sat in front of me
Demanding me to give up what they believed to be an abomination
But we both knew the truth and that it would save the entire nation
Planting this rare seed would take more
than billions out of their hands
So I was never surprised at their obvious panic or demands
First there was his death that they claimed was suicide
I guess he magically tied himself to his own chair
Then cut off and stored his own head in his ride
When he knew they were coming he told me to hide
But it did not take long and they found me
before the end of his funeral song
Shoved in a van and blindfolded in violence
I sat in front of them with nothing to offer but silence
Never saying one word and never making one move
They tortured me for five long months of my life
Yet, I had never been more proud to be my husband's wife
I finally found a way to escape one day but
it never meant that I was free
From that point on I was always on the run
There was no longer a solid home for me
But there in that greenhouse at my journey's end I smiled
Not just at the hundreds of miles but the final victory
I reached into my pocket and took one last look
I kissed the tiny and rare marijuana seed
He told me that it would heal all and this fact the government knew
A century ago they burned any trace of real plants that existed
The pharmacies got richer and kept collecting their dues

But here I stood and here I would stay
To plant this seed and create better days
With one large and final breath I pushed it down into the soil
I watered it quickly just as the guards barged inside
Seizing my body with force to the ground
I smiled with success and pride
As soon as they lifted me off of the ground to be delivered
The ground suddenly broke free and revealed
the largest purple marijuana tree
It even broke through the roof of the greenhouse rapidly
Hovering tall for all to see
Not caring that I was certainly the one to blame
The world would never even be the same
Just as quickly as that one grew, out popped
up another one and then two
Until there were four and hundreds more
They labeled me a rebel, a terrorist, and disgrace
Others would say in the dictionary, the word
"hero" would display my face
Because not too long after, when they all quickly spread
My name and his name...our story remained solid in everyone's head!

"One Day"

They told me to never go near that alley
For me, following directions had always been temporary
What I could not have I always wanted
Things that were easy to obtain I always avoided
My days were filled with dead ends and disappointments
That's what led me there slowly but surely
As if it were a mind game at first, I waited
Never questioning its reason for being avoided
Never questioning its reason for being cursed
Then one day, my life seemed to be at its worst
Bills this, lies that. Rejection this, loneliness is back
So my name was whispered each day that I passed
Softly at first, tickling my ear lobe like the wings of a tiny gnat
I would peer towards the sound then I would take five steps back
I heeded the warnings and ran them over in my head
Yet something just kept right on pushing me towards that direction
Day after day...even at night as I would lie in my bed
So I hesitated the day that I finally decided to go
How could I be so afraid of something that I don't even know?
Moment by moment, it was as if I had no control
I just had to see it. My wisdom had to grow
When I walked upon the alley I immediately felt it
It was uncomfortable and disturbing
Like a fiery burn from a flame
Or the stab of a sharp knife inside of a womb slowly turning

Dark, hopeless, and unwelcoming...I still stepped inside of that alley
One stride at first, then two until I finally made it to the sixth
An icy voice spoke, "We've been waiting for you."
The darkness was like a hot and heavy blanket
Thick in its silence and thick in its depth
Uninviting and cold enough for me to see the clouds of my breath
I could feel another presence there. Standing near me indirectly
I tried to turn and leave but my heavy feet suddenly would not let me
"You're here to discuss your future plans
I am the fix and you are the man
If you tell me all of your desires
I am the *only* one that can take you higher!"
Visions of luxury quickly filled my head
Days of plenty and never again having to beg
Five course meals, beautiful houses, and foreign cars too
Month long vacations, worldly attractions to see and do
It all felt so euphoric. Like a totally lifted weight
Here I stood in front of a faceless and unknown stranger
Some sort of genie that would seal my fate
Without another word, in the darkness, a
set of sharp white teeth grinned
Even in the eeriness of this moment, I felt I had found a friend
Like everything else that had a price, there
were stated terms and conditions
Like the majority of the world...I ignored them completely
Shaking the hand of the faceless man eagerly
Upon leaving the alley, I automatically felt free
As if I held the world in my hands and everyone answered to me
Powerful and confident, everything seemed to come easily
That day there was no stress. There was no anxiety
That day there was no pain
I felt like the greatest king who ever reigned
By the time twenty-four entire hours passed
The excited breaths I was able to breathe were my last
The angel of death came and took me by the hand

He even paid my fare to sail the river of death
Undeniable pity for a shallow and broke ass man
As I drowned in my pride and stupidity
I cried out, "Why just *one* day?!"
My old friend from the alley cackled in amusement
"The terms and conditions were specifically stated."
You wished for a DAY of no problems and no sorrow
A DAY of no stressing, no begging, and never having to borrow
Being the decent soul that I am, for you, I dared not decline
I granted your request and you got what you wanted
In exchange for your soul being mine
Anger consumed me. I knew that I had been tricked
I was the fool that had been fooled. I was a lollipop that was licked
Beat down by undeniable pride, I grew humble and began to beg
I dropped down to my knees and cried, but there
was nothing else that could be said
My cries went unanswered and there was no sympathy for me
Twenty-four hours of ignorance and greed cost my precious eternity
Forevermore demons haunted me; the terrible price I had to pay
All for not listening and losing my faith
And for the worthless comfort of just one day

"It's All Just a Game"

Times of loneliness in a room full of people
Willingness, loyalty, and massaging his ego
All that she asked was a time without others
Time of quality and love from her always busy lover
She tried not to complain. She tried to understand
She was a supportive woman. She let her man be a man
Whenever she would go to him to discuss put aside feelings
She always left with no resolution
She was frustrated and could not find healing
This was a situation she never felt their love would bring
But she stuck it out with abundant patience
She remained a humble queen to her king
Day after day she would imagine he actually cared
That he would recognize her obvious sadness
She prayed that he would step up and be there
His selfish heart would not beat for her
Only for his ambitions and what his kingdom was worth
The rook saw her face and inquired about her tears
He had more than helped the king protect her over many years
She asked for the rook's advice but he seemed a little too on edge
Only telling her not to look back and remain patient with her plight
Only keep moving forward or even to the left or the right
The bishop also noticed her sadness
He was cunning and dared not come at her straight forward
He took in the situation only as far as he could see

Always approaching it sideways and diagonally
He insulted the king and fed her lies of the his dishonest intentions
Of carefully planned secret meetings and
late nights that went unmentioned
He told her that she deserved better and that she deserved more
Even with his gossip and secrets, the king was
still the only one that she yearned for
One day the knight came around in all of his glory
Shining brighter than a diamond in front of her eyes
He told her of his journeys and of his war story
He sent her secret gifts behind the king's
back and poetry that was deep
Trying to convince her that it was her lonely heart he would seek
The queen turned away his advances even after hearing him sing
She knew her situation was quite disappointing
But she still remained a humble queen to her king
The knight finally gave up in frustration
He told her to keep living in her hell
He retreated back to the fields of war
He hurtfully took his L
Now the king still remained consumed
Noticing none of their attempts for her or the efforts
He felt that she would never even think to leave
He felt other than him, there was no one better
So when the pawn began to come around faithfully
He never caught his gaze that constantly rested on his beautiful queen
He never noticed the connection they made so easily
Their lustful nights and meetings went unnoticed
As did their plans and conversations about being together
He never heard the promising words of
giving her a life that was better
As the king drowned in his ego he would never even know
Or realize why the pawn crept through the
darkness of his room one night
Violently murdering his bishop, his rook, and even his knight

He felt that it all peacefully was going his way
But the pawn ran off with his queen in utter and shocking success
Leaving what was once a lavish and thriving
kingdom in a dramatic mess
The queen lived on hidden with him in the
country for five months of loving
Enjoying the pleasant change and attention the pawn seemed to bring
Until the day he murdered her, burying her still half alive
He then raced back to the kingdom, with not one new woman
But five
He murdered the weak and lonely king
Taking over the kingdom and everything it brings
Basking in the glory of his evil fate
It is always wise to check your mate

"Strange Fruit"

Darkness
All that I could see was darkness
All that I could feel was darkness
It covered me like a blanket of comfort
Defining the depths of the night like the color of my skin
Harshly breathing and moist with sweat
I felt cooling breezes from the Louisiana wind
I stumbled around clumsily like a newborn deer
Voices rang out and the barking of hunting dogs were near
Freedom is what they claim we have
Yet here I was, hiding and running like a little boy
Not standing my ground like a grown ass man
"I think that uppity nigger ran this way!
I can smell his ass good and loud
He's gotta learn a lesson tonight!
We'll make him regret running that foul ass mouth!"
Behind large weeping willows and through deep swamps
I crept
If I actually endured this night, it would be one I would never forget
I walked along further towards anywhere else
To a place that I was unsure of
But I just wanted to survive. To strive. To love
I heard noises that sounded like creaking
Faint at first but loud enough to catch it
Not as obvious as my breathing

I strained to discover the source while on my course
Which did not take me long at all
As my brown eyes slowly rose I gasped at the tragic fates
Hanging directly above my nose
I had never seen so many
The shoes of numerous Negro men slowly swung back and forth
A despairing garden of dark human pendulums
With the expectations of adding many more to come
Frozen in terror I already could feel my fate
And something told me that I just might be too late
Being Black and intelligent to them was my greatest sin
I was being hunted like I wasn't shit but prey
The way that I lived my life many days
Being an activist was a dangerous game
And every single one of them knew my name
The dogs and the voices weren't too far now
I crept between my fellow brothers
Thinking on my last thoughts and final vow
"We've got a situation towards the main highway.
Needing all backup available in the area."
Silence filled the trees as curses escaped them
Their flashlights headed the other direction growing dim
"Goddamnit! I know we could have got his ass!"
"Another day Yates. Another day. Tonight, he just got a lucky pass."
"LETS GO BOYS!"
The barking of dogs grew faint as I grew moist
from sweat and the falling rain
God granted me so much more than favor that night
God decided I needed to keep my life
I needed to live to tell this story for others just like you
I immediately left town after that, spreading
my word and the unbiased truth
I smiled warmly as I looked at the dropped
jaws of my three grandchildren

Uncomfortable and interested with questions
that added up to a million
"So, you actually saw the dead bodies hanging?"
"Where would you have hidden if they continued hunting?"
"Did you know any of the men that you saw?"
"Tell us another one Paw-Paw!"
My daughter strolled into the room with a frown
Shaking her pretty head as she looked around
"Daddy you shouldn't be telling them that!
They aren't ready to even know what all of it means"
I grumbled under my breath at her wishes for indiscretion
"They're not too young and I'm teaching them a valuable lesson
Life isn't easy for us and they should always know what that means
It's not like it happened in the times they
tell them in their history books
This was in the year of 2018."

"Watching"

I am standing still
The entire world moves around me
In eloquent waves of calm and peace
Full of more comfort than my world
But I never lived comfortably
I would lie awake in fear and in pain
Slow to even shift my body's position
Taking in the momentary normalcy of the night
Enjoying the sweet bliss of this intermission
I live through long days full of silence and agreed nods
Treading through life through the eyes of someone else
Catering to a vague and painful façade
I can't even remember when it all began
I can't even think of the reason why
In the beginning you never seemed like the type
In the beginning you were a another guy
All of us go through situations
Everyone's past affects them deeply
For some reason I compromised my expectations
Other distractions caused me not to see
One bruise here
One bite mark there
Two pulls to the hair
Three seconds of a deadly stare
And I still chose to live there

Trying to figure out just when the real you would be back
Reflecting on everything now
I know I was insane
Maybe you laced my food with crack
Day after day and moment after moment
You would find something within me
Something so small so skillfully
It just took me longer to realize it was all you
Your heart wasn't at peace
As you pummeled me with your insecurities
Suffocated me with your harsh words
Controlling me
Keeping my spirit caged in like a domestic bird
I told intricate lies for you
I hid your true character with embarrassment
You turned the most beautiful moments into chaos
Even when you were wrong you made sure you still won
Eggshells could never bear this weight
I was the only one that could steer my fate
Something in me tried to convince me of the worst
That maybe this was supposed to be my life
Maybe it was something that I deserved
I was at a place in my life
One that practically made me feel dead
But it seemed like the more that I stayed around you
I began to find reasons to leave you and live
Men all seemed the same to me
Even the actions of you
You never changed my mind when you slapped me around
There was no love or care in any action you would do
Everything I expressed I went through flew out of your window
As if my past was irrelevant or something you didn't know
In secret you were a monster
One of the smallest I had ever seen
But the love I had for you seemed to make it too late

Too late for my mind to intervene
As I sat there constantly repeating
You are more than this. Just leave as soon as you can.
Every attempt turned you more humble
Every time I stepped towards the door you became a better man
Then he would just leave once again
Shedding the shell of decency and emotion
Replacing it with the usual sarcasm and unnecessary commotion
The secrets and the tears
They all stretched into nearly two years
The day you asked me to be your wife
Was when it really hit me
So away from what I knew would be a depressing life
Days filled with voluminous orders and sneers
Misplaced feelings
Rivers and pillows full of tears
Seeing it on television never describes the true vision
Of endless days hoping that bedtime is near
And peaceful enough not to endure any fear
Normal enough just to lay still
In the night
In the darkness
Wondering which parts are even real
Praying to God as you watch yourself
Watching yourself through death's windowsill

V. Life

"The One"

I shine and I glow
Possessing the knowledge to tell you everything you need to know
The world will never be the same
I am the one
Never to be blamed for anything as long as you're having fun
Boosting up your confidence
You are pretty convinced that you couldn't live without me
Not even blessed with the simple ability to tell time
You know I am yours and you are mine
I am the one
Read between all of my lines
Smile as I entertain
Prepared to die at any moment just as quickly as I came
Think of me in the first sun rays of the morning
Laugh with me in the late hours of the night
Our bond is strong and I can do no wrong
It's a fact that I will most certainly be right
I am the way; I am the day, and then some
I promise you I am the one
I can steal your girl
I can cause a riot
Even if I boldly lied right now you'd still buy it
I swear that I am beyond cool
With abundant effect and plenty of pull
Depending on the situation, if you see me you would run

Knowing the history of my damage
You could not manage
I am the one
Leader of all things which carry a purpose
I deserve an upgrade
Sometimes I misbehave but I will still be around
For you to always be saved. Even for you to get paid
I do it better. I do it the worst
How could you be without me?
How would you know all of the gossip first?
Our interactions are necessary
Our interactions are cursed
I swear I am a ton of fun. You can never run
I defy every single odd
Because I am the one
I am your promised alarm and I will pull on the charm
Whether it's legal or illegal I am corrupt
Savage intentions and a few federal secrets that remains unmentioned
Without me you are pushing your luck
I fire shots faster than a gun and I can make you leave or come
Until this world stops spinning I will always be the one
Robbing all of your precious moments
Never leaving you alone
I am what you are most addicted to
I am your cell phone

"Different"

I feel every emotion to the core of my soul
I have impossible definitions to possible goals
Created out of love, I have seen true commitment
If you come for me
If I am what you truly seek
You must know that I am different
I steal the attention of an entire room
My head held high and void of any gloom
My confidence cannot be measured past the solar system
You must try and keep up with my beat
You should learn how to groove to my rhythm
I have a deep past, the same as others do
With the promise to never take my pain out on you
Realize whether you can handle all my inflictions
I am the brightest light in the darkest nights
You must know that I am different
I will never speak a lie to you
Or you play you to the left
I am always loyal to my morals
I always let fate do the rest
Never avoid me like you don't deserve me
Maybe you just never experienced the best
When they speak of a royal vision I am often mentioned
In possession of a crown glowing with intellect and melanin

Stick with me to get the full effect
Living with nothing on my heart but good intentions
Strong enough to balance the world on my shoulders
Bold enough to dare to be different!

"Unwelcome"

Can I be a woman?
Can I display the femininity and sexuality of my soul?
My skin glistening through light like pure flawless gold
Can my hair fall in my face so perfectly?
Sashaying down the street for all to see
A beautiful body for beautiful days
To my hips is how the music sways
My laughter is a jazz song
The way my eyes stare at you is never wrong
The light touches I choose to give are natural
As I converse with you about mythology and my goals
I have unwanted habits and unwanted roles
My body is my temple
Something that I will always know
My mind and my heart is protected and binding
They will never consent to your objectifying
Nor your womanizing stares
I am not just some fat ass you want to squeeze
I am not my breasts nor my hair
I am not your "maybe"
My name is not "baby"
You cannot get a minute of my time
You are not an alien so don't invade my space
I am more than what you see and I am not a race
Know your place because you have one

That place is not to push up on me
That place should not make me feel undressed
Or violated to any degree
I am here to make you see
I am a lady, a queen, a strong one
Calling the shots and doing what I want
With the right to say when you are unwelcome

"Beauty Lies"

Beautiful confusion
Outer visions that display illusions
The physical that we see can withhold spiritual catastrophe
Women often voice descriptive words
Claiming to be "slayed" and "snatched"
Spending their fortunes on temporary masks
But does the spirit even match?
Strutting around like a delusional peacock on display
The physicality of perfection voicing what the soul cannot ever say
It takes work to maintain a façade that is
hidden from the obvious truth
Never knowing the fact that others need to
react to the person inside of you
Cornucopias of makeup won't change the hurt
Designer price tags cannot tell what you're worth
Until you swim the depths to truly accept the beauty that is within
It will continue to be unacceptable to find peace in your natural skin

"The Struggle"

I question the essence of who I am
Maybe I should have been born a man
I can't see the picture clearly enough
My heart beats smooth and my edges are too rough
Emotionally hypersensitive to a world playing pretend
A world where you have to question who really is your friend?
If you ever went broke who would love you for your ends?
And they say the end is always near
But they've been saying that since I was ten
Feeling like the only one genuinely concerned
I can't walk around like the others
No pathway to guide me and no lessons learned
I do not deserve fake
Nor do I deserve the half ass way of anything
When the world chews you up and spits you back out
You can do nothing but find purpose in your suffering
I mean who really cares? Who's really going to be there?
They tell you to trust a brand new situation
But that's how I got here
That's how I became this shell of a queen
That fills her empty spaces with poetry, charities, and giving
Confidently I struggle with compassion and not really giving a shit
About you, what you think, what you want, how you live
Unaware if anything you tell me is even legit
Is it worth it or not?

Do I have a purpose in life or am I someone else's life purpose?
I forgot
So let me write it down and fully think it out
Let me lift you up and then take you the other way around
My skeletons can never be found
They say we all have them in our closets
Does that mean that I can't lock it?
Because I sure as hell can't stop it
It overflows with each year that passes by
Making the right choices should be easy
But I never really knew why
Choices are the hardest part of life
The very options that produce your results
Your cue on whether you should keep words to yourself
Or tell an interesting story or a dirty joke
Whether you should or should not take that last drink
The golden rule is before you do anything you should carefully think
My options are something that I have to shuffle
As my inner thoughts face the hardest struggle